The Global Banquet

Warren Brown

Published by Warren Brown, 2024.

This is a work of fiction. Similarities to real people, places, or events are entirely coincidental.

THE GLOBAL BANQUET

First edition. November 12, 2024.

Copyright © 2024 Warren Brown.

ISBN: 979-8230119487

Written by Warren Brown.

Also by Warren Brown

Christmas Comics
The Father Christmas Factor
Christmas Legacies

Prolific Writing for Everyone
On Writing Magic
Universe of Creativity and Inspiration for Writers
Ocean of Ideas and Inspiration for Writers
Museum of Creativity and Inspiration for Writers
Doorways to Ideas and Inspiration for Writers
The Writer's Creativity Cave
The Writer's Oasis
Castle of Ideas and Inspiration for Writers
Chasm of Creativity and Inspiration For Writers
Island of Creativity and Inspiration for Writers

Standalone
Supernova: A Collection of Science Fiction Short Stories
Instant Poetry App
The Power of the Storyteller- A Collection of Short Stories

Vintage Tales: Eurasian Short Stories
Impostor Assassin
Camelot Crypto 1- Crypto Genesis
Camelot Crypto 2- Crypto Odyssey
Camelot Crypto 3- Crypto Symbiosis
Camelot Crypto: Three Short Crypto-currency Stories
Three Christmas Coins: A Poem
The Christmas Dimension
Happy New Year
Festive Delights
Coulrophobia: Empire of the Clown King
Creative Vibes
Rewrite Your Story To Become The Hero
Pandemic Blasters
New Year Odyssey
Pandemic Blasters Omnibus
Travel Man
Monkey in Mind
Masquerade
The Marauders and Mavericks
Mystic Inspiration Prompts for Writers
Cafe of Creativity and Inspiration For Writers
Quick Guide to Increasing Sales for Your Magnetic E-Book
The Global Citizen
The Mindset for Living in a World with Artificial Intelligence
Crowning of King Kang
Wild Ride
Storyteller's Toolbox
The Shangri-La Vacation
The Halloween Zombie Train
Humane Resources: A.I. Singularity
Civilization Rocks
New Year Magic

Bouquet for Earth
The Global Banquet

Watch for more at https://warren4.wixsite.com/warren.

Table of Contents

....	1
Introduction	3
Sit at the Long Table and Enjoy Community Building Time............	4
Banquet at the Long Table- Table 1	6
Banquet at the Long Table with Superheroes- Table 2	8
Banquet at the Long Table with Barbarians- Table 3..........................	9
Banquet at the Long Table with the Sleuths- Table 4	10
Banquet at the Long Table with Literary Greats- Table 5	11
Banquet at the Long Table with Great Scientists- Table 6................	13
Banquet at the Long Table with Master Chefs- Table 7....................	15
Banquet at the Long Table with Villains and Monsters- Table 8 ...	16
Banquet at the Long Table with Kings and Queens- Table 9...........	18
Banquet at the Long Table with Great Actors and Singers- Table 10..	19
Banquet at the Long Table with Nature- Table 11	20
Banquet at the Long Table with Gods and Goddesses at Olympus- Table 12..	21
Banquet at the Long Table with your Ancestors and Your Descendants- Table 13..	22
The Global Banquet Buffet at the Long Table- Table 14	24
Delights at the Global Banquet Long Table	26
Tofu Time at the Dinner Table	27
Vindaloo and Chicken Stew	28
The Nawab who ate his Kabab...	29
A spoonful of Love, In every delicious dish of Food........................	30
A Sprinkling of Love, Makes a Dish More Delicious.......................	31
The Master Chef who never tires	32
The Christmas Menu	34
The Christmas Banquet...	36
A Banquet of Golden Fruits..	38
New Year's Lunch	40

Anglo-Indian Recipes- Where East and West blend on a dish 42
Fascination with Food 43
Deboned Fish Served in Kolkata 45
Creating Magic in the Kitchen 46
Cut down on processed foods 48
The Screaming Chef 49
The Dinner Invitation 51
The Healthiest Country in the World 53
The Delightful Scrambled Egg 54
The Hungry Food Tourist 56
A Hectic Evening in the Restaurant Kitchen 57
The Banquet that Never Ends 58
The Global Banquet Project 59

This book is dedicated to my parents Joan and Melvyn Brown, who always encouraged me to be an understanding and helpful person. They are in my heart and memory always.

This Poetry Series was inspired by my article," Sit at the Long Table and Enjoy Community Building Time". You are invited to go on this journey, to visit all the long tables with the most sumptuous meals, to give us your comments and to tell us which was your best table.

The Global Banquet

By
Warren Brown

GOLDCOPY INDEPENDENT PUBLISHING
LONDON. UNITED KINGDOM. 2024

Title: The Global Banquet
Author: Warren Brown
Copyright @Warren Brown. London. United Kingdom. 2024
Cover: Created in Canva by Warren Brown. November 2024
Date: 12 November 2024

Introduction

Sit at the Long Table and Enjoy Community Building Time

Some restaurants have the smallest tables. Couples prefer their own tables, as do individuals who enjoy their privacy. When groups of friends, work colleagues, or family members sit at a long table, they appear to have more fun. Single tables appear to be lonelier, as the diner tries to have his or her meal in silence.

Loneliness and isolation are common problems in society. People feel isolated when they do not step out to interact with others, either for work or for recreation, or when they live in remote places or work from home for long periods of time.

Most dining tables in homes have four to six seats, while others can seat ten to twelve people. Like the ones attached to meeting and conference rooms, in schools, universities and offices. Lunchrooms, in canteens for schools, colleges and workplaces, usually have longer tables to accommodate the staff of departments or particular working areas. I am sure an elaborate study can be done on the length and seating arrangements, as well as patterns formed around long dining tables. Prisons and military dining halls are similarly equipped with long lunch tables, as are schools and universities. This is done to enable an active interaction between the people at every table. The benefit of long tables is that people get to know other people, from different departments or sections, they would have, otherwise, not had the opportunity to meet for engaging conversations.

I believe that sitting at a long table does help to encourage a sense of community, and belonging and does boost the morale of the team to a great degree. However, the opposite would also be true, being that rumours are also passed around these tables like delicious cheese.

A long table brings people with their ideas, and different perspectives together to have a meal. Sharing a meal with others at a long table does help a person feel less isolated and lonely.

Would you prefer to sit at a long table or still enjoy the privacy of your small table? Some of us would love to participate and eat a meal at a global banquet. At the global feast we have the opportunity to taste food from around the world, while meeting the most interesting people, as we have engaging conversations, about customs, traditions, myths, legends and everything that makes us all different, yet the same in so many human ways, as we explore the mysteries of life and our journey through this amazing experience of life.

Banquet at the Long Table- Table 1

Today, you are being invited to attend,
    A banquet at a very long table.
You are today's special guest at this feast.
Your attendance is needed to say the least.
There are many banquets taking place today.
You are invited to choose your special one.
It can be one filled with villains and saints,
Or a long table with Kings and Queens in the Sun.
There are many banquets in this world.
At every long table, great men and women sit.
Some tables will have geniuses and buffoons.
While there are others with villains who sing tunes.
Perhaps you will choose a table you like,
One with people you can agree with today.
You can sit at a new table every single day.
This is your destiny and your dice to play.

This Poetry Series was inspired by my article," Sit at the Long Table and Enjoy Community Building Time". You are invited to go on this journey, to visit all the long tables with the most sumptuous meals, to give us your comments and to tell us which was your best table.

Writing Prompt: You are welcome to write an article about your best long table, why you liked it and what questions you would have asked if you met a person at your long table, who you have long admired or would have wanted to meet. Please link to this article, so that others can go on this journey to the long tables I have created for you to enjoy.

Choose the next Long Table and continue the Adventure today.

Banquet at the Long Table with Superheroes- Table 2

THERE IS A BANQUET at a long table today.
    This is a feast for superheroes with special powers.
    Some can create worlds and universes,
    While others can turn into angels and flowers.
    Welcome to the banquet of superheroes.
    Here the heroes and heroines sit down every day.
    Making the world a better and more positive place.
    They stop asteroids and missiles in outer space.
    You can sit beside your favourite superheroes.
    Sit beside Batman, Superman, or the Flash.
    Wherever you sit and have your super meal,
    You can sit and eat the very best, without the cash.
    Sitting with superheroes and superheroines,
    May make you a superhero with powers too.
    Whatever your gifts, strengths and skills may be,
    You are still a superhero from now till eternity.

Banquet at the Long Table with Barbarians- Table 3

The long table for the feast of the barbarians,
Is filled with meats of all sizes, shapes and designs.
There are fruits, dancing girls, and minstrels' songs,
There are strange musical sounds as they drink their wine.
The swords, daggers, and shields lie on the stone floor,
Pieces of chewed bone are tossed from the boar.
The floor is covered with the remnants of leftovers,
As more wine and dishes of food are brought over.
There is more wine and food than Kind Midas ate.
The music, dancers, jesters, and magicians entertain.
Warriors wrestle in the evening till late at night.
While the barbarian Kings and Queens watch in delight.
You are a guest at this long table for barbarians.
Stay a while and enjoy this rich and luxurious feast.
Converse with the worst and the best barbarians.
You could also meet, King Conan the Cimmerian.

Banquet at the Long Table with the Sleuths- Table 4

There is a banquet at the long table tonight.
There is also intrigue and mystery in the air.
The world's most popular detectives are invited,
To be present at this great feast on crime solving.
You have been invited to be a very special guest.
As an invitee and friend, there is no crime test.
You have Sherlock Holmes and Watson sitting down.
Miss Marple and Poirot are enjoying wine and roast.
Real and fictional detectives enjoy their hearty meal,
As they try to solve a murder and a broken seal.
Everyone present is using their great grey cells.
This is something Sherlock and Watson know so well.
Father Brown, Rosemary Boxer, and Richard Castle,
Licks their lips as the French cuisine is served.
Nancy drew, Miss Marple and Veronica Powers,
Look for clues in the dust under the stars.
The meatballs and sausage, the cheeses and the salads,
It is a delightful culinary experience enjoyed for hours.
You are invited to partake of this heavenly spread.
Spend time and chat away with your favourite sleuth.
Meet Philip Trent, Kyoko Kirigiri and Ellery Queen,
As they solve a crime or a case never heard of or seen.
Watch as Patrick Jane and Beverly Gray eat a Turkish delight,
While Sherlock smokes his cigar in the pale moonlight.

Banquet at the Long Table with Literary Greats- Table 5

THE GREATEST WRITERS and literary giants are invited,
To the banquet feast at the great long table.
You have Charles Dickens, William Shakespeare, and Tolstoy,
Eating delicious meals and discussing their next great works.
Chaucer, and Huxley, enjoy the roasted potatoes and vegetables.
While Orwell, Cervantes, and Homer, enjoy dishes and fables.
Jane Austen and Oscar Wilde, enjoy delicious roasted meats,
Plato and Dante plunge into the depths of their moussaka.
The vegetable tagine and pasta Alla Norma are great delights,
Which brings great ideas into the minds of writers like luminous lights.
Hermann Melville and Gustave Flaubert enjoy their salmon and watercress,
As the beautiful Madame Bovary arrives having forgotten her evening dress.
Proust, Gabriel Marquez, and Murasaki Shikibu, enjoy the duck,
Placed on a large platter filled with spicy vegetables and greens.
You can have the opportunity to converse with these great minds,
To discuss their writing styles and the characters they created in stories.
Enjoy your time at this banquet at the large table with food and wine.

This is the most memorable moment in your life that can last for all time.

Banquet at the Long Table with Great Scientists- Table 6

The scientists of yesterday, today, and tomorrow,
Have all been invited to the feast at the long table?
The banquet has been prepared as a celebration,
For those who thought differently in every situation.
Large strides in science have made progress possible,
Humanity, man, and woman can go wherever they will.
Archimedes drops a grape into his glass of wine,
He knows the Archimedes principle will go beyond time.
Isaac Newton picks up an apple from a bowl of fruits,
It brings back fond memories of gravity the law he created.
Ada Lovelace and Marie Curie share a joke as they sip on wine.
The scientists are feasting on their accomplishments over space and time.
Charles Darwin and Albert Einstein devour their bowl of spaghetti.
While Galileo and Nikola Tesla enjoy their appetizers.
There are scientists like Hawkins and others present,
Who enjoy the dishes from all around the world.
Meatballs, sausages, and chicken breast are relished.
Lamb biryani and chicken tikka are equally relished.
Would you join this table of scientists old and new?
Perhaps your brilliance will also shine right through.
You could speak to Albert Einstein and his relativity,
As Edison converses about the gift of electricity.
The conversations at the large science table are illuminating.

The dinner goes on through the night with the geeks dancing.

Banquet at the Long Table with Master Chefs- Table 7

The master chefs have assembled from around the world.
Everyone is an expert in so many tasty and delightful dishes.
To sit at this long table is the wish of every food enthusiast.
The first dish is a delight and it soon fades as the next one comes.
Every dish is so much more delicious than the last one.
You could eat dishes till the Moon says hello to the Sun.
Welcome to the banquet at the long table,
Make sure that you are ready to eat the meal of your life.
There are dishes from every continent in the world.
The culinary extravaganza has dishes of all types of meat.
There are delicious foods from the Far East.
Every appetizer served is part of a bigger feast.
The master chefs are experts in their craft,
Each has earned his or her stars from great dishes.
Every chef has his or her special signature dish,
That ranges from seafood to chicken, lamb, pork, and fish.
The colours on the plate are so wonderful to behold,
The food must always be eaten steaming hot and never cold.
Would you join this table of culinary mastery,
To eat every delicious ham, croissant, and pastry?
Every dish is served with the guest in mind.
There are so many varieties, that it boggles the mind.
Tell us about your wonderful experience at the long table.
How every dish is so delicious and so very palatable.

Banquet at the Long Table with Villains and Monsters- Table 8

The long table has been prepared for a special banquet.
    It is a feast for all the world's villains and monsters.
There are the fictional ones and the real ones present.
Some only hunt their prey with their scent.
Every villain present is ready for this deadly delicious feast.
The tastier the dishes do bring out the very beast.
Lex Luthor gives a toast to his fellow criminals.
While the Joker makes plans as he eats his steak rare.
The Penguin shares some information about salmon and fish,
While Harley Quinn crushes some berries in her fist.
The villains of comic books have their special tastes,
They eat almost everything so there is no waste.
The Werewolf and the Vampires drink the red wine,
As they tear off the portions of meat, tender and rare.
There is so much food on the dishes and the plates,
There is not much room for fruits, like strawberries and grapes.
Every villain, monster, and ghoul have a great appetite,
They love to eat and to frighten their victims.
They and their food are not a very pretty sight.
Would you sit at this deadly table with murderers and villains?
There are killers and bad seeds from all over the globe.
There are villains and demons from the past, the present and the future,

THE GLOBAL BANQUET

Do you think that you would be comfortable here, at these long tables?

The invitation to the long banquet table is for you if you want,
Feast on wild hares, chickens, turtles, squid, and octopus.
Sit with the villains, from myths, legends, and fables.

Banquet at the Long Table with Kings and Queens- Table 9

The long table for the Royal banquet is prepared.
The best chefs have been hired to prepare amazing dishes.
Every plate and bowl of food is served in silver and gold wares.
The cutlery, the crockery, and the serving platters are beyond comparison.
There are dishes of chicken, lamb, duck, venison steak.
There are Indian, Swedish, and continental dishes complex and rare.
All the food served looks so sumptuous and is fit for Kings.
The table is occupied with Pharaohs, Emperors, Queens, and Kings.
There are kings from India from Ashoka and Chandragupta Maurya.
Emperors of Japan, Jimmu, and Suizei are radiant as the rising Sun.
King Gija and Bu, are deep in conversation with Pharoah Khufu.
Henry the Eighth is enjoying his large dish of wild boar stew.
You are welcome to sit at this royal long banquet table,
To have conversations of Kings, Emperors, and Queens today.
Sip the best wine and beer as you eat the meal set for a King.
If you shower your praises, you may get gold coins and a ring.

Banquet at the Long Table with Great Actors and Singers- Table 10

There is music all around as you walk towards the long table.
The best singers and actors, past, present, and future are here.
The banquet is filled with culinary delights of tasty and extravagant food.
Everything looks so appetizing and tastes equally good.
Zeenat Aman, Merle Oberon and Rekha, sip red wine.
Elvis Presley, Buddy Holly, and Shakira created a new tune.
Charlton Heston and Yul Brynner speak about their latest movie about chess.
Fred Astaire and Ginger Rogers dance, as Humphrey Bogart eats an Eton mess.
Charlie Chaplin and James Dean, eat their chicken roast and potatoes,
While Bob Hope and Sammy Davis Junior, savour a piece of Shepherd's Pie.
Frank Sinatra and Ingrid Bergman enjoy their Thai beef salad dish.
Vivien Leigh and Grace Kelly enjoy, their calamari and boiled fish.
You are invited to this great long table and this amazing feast.
Meet some of the world's greatest screen icons and music legends.
You may be star-struck and you may even get an autograph or two.
Enjoy the banquet with this invitation that is especially for you.

Banquet at the Long Table with Nature- Table 11

There are butterflies and roses at the long banquet table.
The most beautiful horses and a white stallion are at the table.
The best food from around the world is served by nature here.
There are apples from Spain, Wine from Italy and Greece here.
There are lions and tigers with some zebras and rhinos.
The love birds and the peacocks strike a fashion pose.
The freshest fruits, leaves, and twigs so tender are served.
Nature is alive, protected, cared for and always preserved.
The purest waters from the coolest fountains are served.
Avocados, mangoes, lemons, and pineapples are neatly arranged.
Every dish has the sweetest and the ripest fruits for pure delight.
The grapes, the apples, and the bananas shine in the golden light.
You are invited to this great feast at the long table with nature.
The best fruits, vegetables, and salads are served over here.
Take this opportunity to bond and celebrate with nature today.
Mother Nature never lets you down, come what may.

Banquet at the Long Table with Gods and Goddesses at Olympus- Table 12

The long banquet table for the Gods and Goddesses is ready.
They arrive with all their attendants to this large feast.
There are Egyptian, Aztec, Nordic, Incan, and Indian Deities.
Every God and Goddess known to humanity is at the feast.
Wine, ambrosia, and dishes from all the continents are served.
Every culture has its best dishes prepared and devoutly served.
Thor and Neptune eat a delicious meal of lamb and wild boar.
Japanese and Celtic Gods enjoy their meals close to the open door.
San Choi Bau, noodles, and pasta are served warm to the Gods.
Salmon, crabs, prawns, and lobsters are served with its rich sauce.
Lamb Biryani and chicken tikka masala is a delight for the Goddesses.
Every meal known is served as per the Gods' requests and wishes.
You are welcome to sit at the long banquet table with these Gods.
If you have lived a good and honest life, you may even get some rewards.
Take this opportunity to share this heavenly meal of delight.
You will be rewarded with the tastiest food and with radiant light.

Banquet at the Long Table with your Ancestors and Your Descendants- Table 13

Some people love to have meals with family and friends they meet.

What if there was a special long banquet table of your ancestors?

A large banquet table with a feast of all those of your family, past and present.

Where generations of your family have an opportunity to once again meet.

The best wine and beer is served and the best champagne too.

The world's best chefs have prepared the dishes for each member present.

This is a miraculous opportunity for you from Heaven's Sent.

Enjoy the duck, chicken, and pork roast with its lovely aroma and scent.

There are rice dishes, delicious pasta, and couscous like honey to the lips.

The most delicious desserts are served in the most wonderful presentations.

The seafood that is served is so tasty that it will bring a tear to your eyes.

Equally good are the Greek, Italian, and African dishes and so are the pies.

Would you accept this invitation to meet your past and future generations?

You could be eating a meal with your Great-Great-Great Grandfather, at the long table.

You could share a Baklava or an ice-cream sundae with your Great-great-granddaughter.

What would be the best parts of this experience with your family for you to share?

The Global Banquet Buffet at the Long Table- Table 14

There is a wide array of dishes,
   At the global banquet table.
There are delicious dishes from Egypt,
Silver bowls filled with culinary delights,
From Spain, Greece, Africa and Portugal.
Wherever you look you will find,
Tasty delights to blow your tastebuds,
To thrill and exhilarate your mind.
The dishes are laid out on the long tables,
On shiny new dishes with elaborate designs.
There are champagne flutes of every kind.
With bottles of the best and finest wines.
Every individual who sits at this global banquet,
Can eat as much as he or she would like.
The plates and bowls will suit every palate.
There is no distinction between the rich and the poor.
Every person is an equal at the global banquet.
Every human being has the right and the seat,
To taste whatever, they want to feast and to eat.
There are delicious delicacies from Holland and Ireland,
With great meals from China, Japan, India and England.
Every country, state, region from around the globe,
Is represented with its dishes at the global banquet.
You are invited to sit at this great and precious feast.

THE GLOBAL BANQUET

To share your stories with the others at this table.
To exchange thoughts about cultures, myths and traditions.
An opportunity to become one with the rest of humanity,
A chance to advance your mind, imagination and creativity.
There is nothing more important in the world,
Then a selection of great dishes from around the world,
To come together with so many who want to share,
Conversations for change, and growth that are beyond compare.
Come to this global banquet and share your stories,
Your food, your customs, your ideas and your tales.
The global banquet is open to all of humanity,
Feast, enjoy, live, love and share your time,
To all who sit at this table with food and wine.

Delights at the Global Banquet Long Table

Tofu Time at the Dinner Table

Some people love it while others don't,
    Some people eat it and others just won't.
Some people do not even have a clue,
What is the strange food called tofu?
Tofu is a popular plant and meat-based alternative.
It is soya which is rich in proteins in the form of tofu.
There are a variety of dishes one can prepare,
Some are culinary delights and others so rare.
Tofu is a great source of protective antioxidants,
It is known to alleviate menopausal symptoms too.
Tofu supports the good health of a beating heart.
It is a plant protein and supports blood sugar levels too.
Prepare some tofu in your home today,
Serve it to your family and watch them smile.
Add this rich protein to their diet plan,
As only a caring and loving chef like you can.

Vindaloo and Chicken Stew

Boy! Boy! Bring it all to me now,
    Chicken curry and pulao,
Bring out the silver spoon,
From my Aunty June,
And let us eat that tasty chicken chow.
Let us have an entertaining talk,
as I use my silver spoon and fork.
"I want to eat some warm rice, vindaloo,
prawn curry and chicken stew,"
As we have an engaging talk,
And listen to music around the clock.

The Nawab who ate his Kabab

Rudolf lived like a wealthy Nawab
    On peas pulao, chicken tikka and spicy Kabab,
Since his cook prepared a tasty paste
Rudolf developed an avid taste,
Then he was crowned King of the "Kabab".
Young Charlie went to the beach at Puri
Living on hot spicy potato curry and dal-puri,
So when he returned from his long trip,
On a cargo-laden ship, he dived into the sea,
Saving himself as he swam in tomato puree.
Old man Smith from some unheard-of-land,
Built his house upon the shifting sand,
Whenever he would go to his shop,
His wife would prepare him tasty potato chop,
They opened up their homecooked food shop.

A spoonful of Love, In every delicious dish of Food

A spoonful and a sprinkling of love,
Can create a buffet of great dishes,
Fulfilling every foodie's heartfelt wishes.
Stir that pot and cook it well,
Let the pot rise and swell,
With all the love that you include,
In every delicious dish of food.

A Sprinkling of Love, Makes a Dish More Delicious

When Mum prepared her meals,
    She always put that extra sprinkle.
A sprinkling of love with every meal,
Which made all her dishes taste like magic,
Delicious, enjoyable and it set happiness free.
As you prepare a meal of one or three,
For yourself and your family,
Add that special ingredient,
A sprinkling of magical love set free,
To make it delicious and tasty.
Preparing a meal is magical,
When all the elements are blended,
To form a complete and appetizing dish,
One that satisfies our hunger and culinary wish.
A spoon full and a sprinkling of love,
Can create a buffet of great dishes,
Fulfilling every foodie's heartfelt wishes.
Stir that pot and cook it well,
Let the pot rise and swell,
With all the love that you include,
In every delicious dish of food.

The Master Chef who never tires

There was one mega food truck in town,
　　It served the best food for miles around.
Whatever the weather and whatever the day,
The best food was served, as warm as the day.
You could get the best price on all the meals,
It was the best mega food truck on wheels.
It provided the best food with the sweetest deals,
For office workers, the public, and the well-heeled.
If anyone told you the food was no good,
They were definitely a pack of wolfish liars,
That never tasted the food from those fires.
The Chef always whipped up a perfect storm,
Of ingredients, meats, and spices galore,
That was a festivity of culinary delights,
That would leave anyone begging for more.
The Chef was a master at his burning fires,
He added the spices to his dishes in haste,
Wonderfully blended meals from snacks to paste.
Burgers, chips, chicken drumsticks peppery hot,
With soups, tacos, noodles, fried rice was what you got.
The fame of that "Mega Food Truck" spread far,
To the heads of companies and to the drinks bar.
People travelled from far and wide to have a meal,
At the best food truck that was on hot wheels.
The kitchen was always in the middle of a food storm,

With the super Chef who never tires,
While preparing the best food in town,
That was popular for miles around.
Where is that mega food truck you say?
It disappeared from the street the other day.

The Christmas Menu

The festive season is close at hand. Have you prepared the shopping list for your Christmas menu? If you have not done so yet, you are not the only one. There are so many people, who are busy and have not yet completed their Christmas shopping, for clothes, gifts, the Christmas tree, decorations, and all the items needed for the Christmas meal.

There are some people who are ready for Christmas well in advance. With a few individuals making lists and preparations from October. Do you happen to be one of these people or are you more like the person who rushes around getting things together at the last minute?

Several families have the Christmas tree and decorations all in place in the first week of December. While there are families who prefer to do the decorations on Christmas Eve. We do the decorations at home in the first week of December. However, Mum and Dad preferred getting the home ready for Christmas during Christmas week, with the final touches completed on Christmas Eve or on Christmas morning.

Christians all over the world celebrate Christmas. The Christmas meal, lunch, or dinner is the most important family meal and everyone tries to place the best Christmas dishes on the table, depending on culture and geographical location. Families in the West prefer a chicken or turkey roast with all the trimmings and side dishes to complete the Christmas meal. Families in other parts of the world have their special festive dishes served on Christmas Day.

What is the family Christmas meal tradition at your home and when do you start preparing the meal, on the day, or the day before, depending on the size of your family? Have a delicious Christmas meal, this festive season.

The Christmas Banquet

The large banquet table is served,
　　With the best dishes from across the land,
For people who have crossed rivers,
From people who have crossed desert sand.
Come one, come all to the Christmas banquet,
Come and have delicious food and wine,
As we celebrate this wonderful Christmas time.
The variety of dishes represents the world,
Some sweet, others savory, the choice is yours,
To pick the most appetizing dishes on the menu.
You could have a roasted duck with sauce,
Or fried prawns and fish in the batter so spicy,
Or dishes from far off Russia and India,
From the far reaches of Africa and China.
There were Christmas dishes of great variety,
From lands far and wide, over land and sea.
Come one, come all to the Christmas banquet,
Come and have delicious food and wine,
As we celebrate this Christmas time.
The Christmas banquet is open to all,
To eat the best dishes to their heart's content.
Friendship, brotherhood, peace, and unity,
Was the spirit of Christmas at the table,
And around the decorated Christmas tree.
Come and sit at the Christmas banquet,

THE GLOBAL BANQUET

It is the best way to have a Merry Christmas,
It is the best way to celebrate,
The birth of the saviour on Earth,
With Christmas joy, peace, and mirth.
The Christmas banquet is served,
A feast for all mankind and humanity,
A celebration so well deserved,
To be enjoyed in peace, love, and unity.
Come one, come all to the Christmas banquet,
Come and have delicious food and wine,
As we celebrate this Christmas time.

A Banquet of Golden Fruits

As a child, he saw fruits of gold,
    Growing on the orchard trees at home.
Those fruits were wonderful to hold,
Apples, pears, oranges, and cherries,
They were the wealth of his family he was told.
That orchard of golden fruit on silver trees,
Was his paradise of treasure swaying in the breeze.
He watched the sunshine on the fruits,
As a teenager, he helped his father on the fields,
To collect the fresh fruits of the orchard trees,
As they swayed gently in the summer breeze.
As a man, he cultivated his fruits and crops,
He cleared his land after every harvest with his plough.
He planted new seeds and watched them grow,
They gave a great yield and some more.
That orchard of golden fruits on golden trees,
Were the wealth and the treasure of his family.
For generations, his family tilled the soil,
It was his family's livelihood and paradise,
They were rewarded with the fruits of their toil.
That orchard of golden fruit on silver trees,
Was his paradise of treasure swaying in the breeze.
The difficult times were when he worked hardest,
To protect his land from snow, frost, and ice,
To save the crops from rodents, pests, and lice,

To enable the orchard to always deliver its best.
He thanked the Heavens for a bounty of a harvest,
Overcoming famines was the hardest test.
The family orchard, its golden fruits, and silver trees,
Held the wealth and its legacies in its leaves in the breeze.
He always rescued his orchard and there was no price,
It was his soil, his home, his legacy, and his paradise.

New Year's Lunch

The New Year lunch was special,
    The family, relatives, and friends,
They were waiting patiently for it to arrive.
Where was the New Year lunch?
Was it on the way, they wondered?
It was going to be a delicious selection,
The food was going in one direction.
The food baskets were all prepared,
Then, suddenly the lights went out,
The stoves stopped working,
She was frantic as she rushed about.
Lisa was stumped and she knew,
That the food would never get prepared,
She was sinking into a bowl of chicken stew.
Lisa phoned the families on her list,
She told them that the food would not arrive.
They were all furious and gave her the second degree,
For not delivering the New Year lunch,
As they sat grumbling around the Christmas tree.
Lisa told them that she had a surprise in store.
So, she called her friends around,
Prepare trays and trays of delicious sarnies.
The sandwiches were a huge hit,
With all the members of every family,
After they gave Lisa the second degree.

This was a different New Year spread,
Made with slices of surprises on bread.
The New Year lunch was never the same,
Perhaps, "the second degree" was to blame.

Anglo-Indian Recipes- Where East and West blend on a dish

Anglo-Indian cookery has developed by leaps and bounds over the past four hundred years. Anglo-Indian recipes were passed down from mother to daughter in the Anglo-Indian community over the years.

These Anglo-Indian recipes are unique to the community, that originated in India four centuries ago. The names and ingredients of a lot of the dishes have been adopted and remodelled over the years by Indian restauranteurs to suit the Western palate.

My mother Joan was a wonderful chef and prepared some of the tastiest Anglo-Indian dishes, which were enjoyed and loved by family and friends. Mum inspired me to cook Anglo-Indian food.

Fascination with Food

That vital component of life that makes living beings, plants and animals enjoy this life on Earth, is food. The fruits, vegetables, meats, poultry, and all that we consume give us the energy to fulfil our destiny.

I have always been fascinated with food, since childhood. I would get up in the morning and look forward to the delicious meals Mum would prepare. My mother was a great chef, and she would prepare culinary wonders for the family, relatives and friends. My mum introduced me to shopping for fresh meat and vegetables. I still look forward to shopping for groceries every week.

I have always been an observer of life. My dad always told me that observation is the key to understanding life. As a child, I was more interested in eating tasty food. As a teenager, I was curious to see how Mum would prepare her food. As an adult, Mum told me to pay closer attention to her cooking methods, as it would help me later in life.

Today, I enjoy cooking dishes as much as I enjoy shopping for fruits, vegetables, and meats, as my wife and I put them all together to prepare dishes to eat and relish. Cooking is like science, where a lot of materials are put together, with spices and placed on a fire to combine them into a delicious preparation. There are materials, a recipe, a method, and an end product when the process is completed.

It is always important to pay attention and appreciate the food we eat in life, as it will then have a positive effect on our bodies. There are some people who consume food, without paying attention to what they are eating and so it is not properly digested by their bodies.

I like visualizing food as energy blocks that we consume, which in turn is absorbed by our bodies to release the energy we need to fulfil everyday activities in the world. Appreciate the food that you eat and watch the way your life is transformed from the way you think to the way you view the world and work.

Deboned Fish Served in Kolkata

I am not a fan of cooked fish, though I have tried to be over the years. My Mum prepared some delicious fish preparations. My wife loves to prepare fish as well. My favourite is fish and chips. I love the fried fish in batter and the generous serving of fried potato chips.

In the city of Kolkata in India, there is a great surprise in store for fish lovers. A restaurant in Kolkata has prepared the first-ever deboned fish delicacies. This will be a paradise for every fish lover in the city. Imagine not having to remove those delicate and sharp bones, before you have a mouthful of the fish curry. Imagine being able to enjoy the full flavour of the fish cooked in spices without having to chew a bone. Imagine being in fish heaven eating the best fish, free of bones.

Perhaps when I visit the city later, I might visit the restaurant to taste these amazing deboned fish preparations. Have you prepared a deboned fish preparation and would you get the same enjoyment? Some people love eating fish, because of all the bones, that add to the flavour of the curry. The food gods must be either annoyed or over the moon, with these new culinary creations of deboned fish curries.

Creating Magic in the Kitchen

Sue Ellen had big cooking plans,
    As she arranged her pots and pans.
She needed to get her menu right,
With all the vegetables and meat in sight.
Today was a big day for her family,
It was her son's 21st birthday party.
Sue Ellen needed to get everything right,
From the roast to the ice cream delight.
All the relatives and friends were coming,
Including cousin Rachel who thought she could sing.
No one was looking to lovely Rachel's solo,
Including Uncle Jim who would always snore.
Harry was going to be twenty-one,
He was her beloved eldest son.
Sue Ellen was busy in her large kitchen,
As the guests arrived, all stormed in.
The most delicious food she was preparing,
The fried rice was cooking, and the soup needed stirring.
In a bowl were the roasted brown succulent potatoes,
As the aroma of food seductively wafted up every nose.
The fried sausages, mash potatoes, turkey and peas,
Looked as delicious as the hog roast and spicy curry.
Sue Ellen and her husband Dan were beaming and proud,
As the family photos were taken with the large crowd,
While the energetic music played so loud.

Harry was going to be a famous physician,
While her son Gerry was going to be a musician.
Sue Ellen was the greatest chef and a magician,
With the delicious food magically made in her kitchen.

Cut down on processed foods

France is cutting down on the nitrites,
    The one put in foods to make them last longer.
They can cause the serious disease of cancer,
Which will make you weaker and not stronger.
Cut down on all that processed food,
It is not good for your health in the long run,
It is as dangerous as a smoking gun.
Hopefully, other countries will follow suit,
To give all those nitrites a good boot.
Processed foods are the rage worldwide,
We love the taste and they look good,
Watch your appetite and knock on wood.
We all love to have tasty and delicious food.
Limit the amount of processed food you eat,
Packed will all those nitrates and nitrite.
They do not just make the meat look good,
They will not keep you healthy or at ease,
Keep away from all those nitrates and nitrite,
To remain happy, healthy and so bright.

The Screaming Chef

The kitchen was in a state,
    Wherever he looked he saw,
A used spoon and a dirty plate.
The Chef was screaming,
At the top of his voice,
He was not used to seeing a mess.
He loved to see a clean kitchen,
He loved cleanliness and perfection,
Without the tiresome stress.
The young attendants trembled,
In panic and in fear.
They started cleaning up with speed,
Before the chef prepared the next feed.
The chef kept on screaming,
At the top of his voice,
As he watched his attendants,
Wash, scrub, and clean the kitchen.
They now knew without a reasonable doubt,
That the Michelin Star chef loved perfection.
The kitchen was scrubbed, and it was clean.
The meat and vegetables were cut,
By the assistants who were now so keen.
The chef came and with his magic touch,
He prepared a meal fit for Kings,
There were soups, salads, roasts, and bread,

There was duck, pudding, and roasted chicken wings.
The chef now was happy and satisfied,
He could even dance, smile and sing,
As he prepared a meal fit for a King.
The screaming chef loved his kitchen,
As much as he loved preparing food with perfection.

The Dinner Invitation

Hector and his family,
 Were excited that evening.
There was laughter, dancing and singing.
Hector felt like a lottery ticket winner.
His wife Hilary and his two small children,
Were invited out to a very special dinner.
Hector's boss Viktor,
Invited the family to his home,
To have a meal and spend time,
To eat delicious dishes,
While drinking fine wine.
Viktor was a good boss,
He was the ideal type of guy,
Polite, respectful, and upright.
A kind boss who would comfort,
His employees if he saw them cry.
Hector's two little children Jack and Mary,
Ate all the food on their plates,
They even tried the custard and dates.
Hector and Viktor chatted and laughed,
While their wives Hilary and Rebecca,
Spent the evening discussing their lives,
As friends, companions, lovers, and wives.
After a hearty meal Hector and his family,
Left Viktor's home happy and bright,

They all had a good sleep that night.
It was only the next day,
When Hector went into work,
He found his life thrown into disarray,
Viktor and the company had moved away.
Hector had to rebuild his life once again,
He became a driver on an electric train.

The Healthiest Country in the World

There is a country in the world that is the healthiest one, with people enjoying a long life expectancy and very low obesity. Would you live in such a country if one existed? Yes, the country where people can live longer is Japan.

Japan has a marvellous transport network, with low levels of air pollution as well as low obesity rates. The Japanese diet is high in proteins with people eating small portions of food. One resident lived to be 119 years old in Japan.

However, if you do not want to travel as far as Japan, you could always live in the second healthiest country in the world, which is Switzerland.

The healthiest country in the world has a long-life expectancy and extremely low obesity (msn.com)

Prompt: Would you like to live longer and how do you intend to spend all those extra years that you accumulate as a healthy person living to be over a hundred years old?

I would like to live to be old and grey though not to be a hundred. I would use my extra years as a healthy person with a long-life expectancy to do more of my writing work while spending quality time with friends and family. Also, I am intrigued to see what the future holds for humanity in the fields of science and technology.

You are welcome to respond to this writing prompt and I am curious to know why you would like to live to be a hundred years old and what you plan to do with all those extra years, as a healthy individual.

The Delightful Scrambled Egg

Scrambled egg on toast is a favourite for breakfast in Britain. I love scrambled eggs though not always on toast. An egg can be prepared in so many wonderful ways and one of them happens to be the scrambled egg dish. To prepare this simple dish either one, two or several eggs are cracked, salt, and a little water can be added, it is all whisked to make a liquid, that is emptied into a hot pan of oil, to sizzle and become a delicious preparation. I think this is the fastest, the quickest and the easiest way to make a scrambled egg. What is your best way to make a scrambled egg and do you have toast with it or do you prefer a few slices of bread and butter or a roti or a naan bread with it, with a slice of ham or some cheese and mushrooms?

An idea can take on some forms, just like one can prepare a simple egg into several dishes from a fried egg to a poached egg to an egg curry. There are always so many ways to view an idea and it is all in the mind, the creativity and the imagination of the creator. An interior decorator will put the design of an egg in a creative presentation on wallpaper, while a cartoonist, will breathe life into the caricature of an egg, while an animator will give that same egg, a name, a voice and a character to go with it.

Have you got an idea today that you can present in a variety of ways? I took the word "scramble" and created several short articles from that one word. It is always good to brainstorm every idea you get to look at the same thing from different perspectives and you will be surprised at the number of ideas that can be created from that one "seed" idea. Try scrambling every idea you get from now on and you will have a plethora of new stories that you can create. If you like scrambled eggs or not, it is time to prepare yourself a scrambled idea that will give the world a great new story or creation.

The Hungry Food Tourist

All that food looked so delicious,
He was just waiting to sit down,
To have a long and delightful feast.
John was a culinary tourist,
He travelled from East to West,
Eating the dishes of the world,
Was what he always loved the best.
He tasted dishes from around the globe,
From India, China, Thailand, and Spain,
From Venezuela to the African plain.
John was the hungry food tourist,
Making the food videos he loved best.
On every trip, he had a new girlfriend,
Not every girl could tolerate his eating,
Every dish in existence is food without end.
He tasted the best of world cuisine,
Some rare dishes he had never before seen.
His eyes would light up with pure delight,
As new dishes appeared in his hungry sight.
He was fortunate to find on YouTube one day,
Sarah the food blogger with food on her mind,
A better lover and soulmate he would never find.
They travel the world with their growing family,
Living, loving, and enjoying everything culinary.

A Hectic Evening in the Restaurant Kitchen

The restaurant was very busy and all the tables were full. There were queues of people lined up outside the large restaurant. It was Lucy's restaurant. It belonged to her family, and it was now under her management and ownership. Furthermore, it was an Italian family-run restaurant and well known for its perfect home-cooking.

Today, this Friday, was not a perfect day for Lucy. She was working furiously in the kitchen and managing it was well. The Chef had fallen sick. Today, was an important day for the restaurant, as the Mayor of the Town with the Town Council were attending a campaign celebration. Lucy wanted everything to be perfect. There were a few dishes that were returned to the kitchen because the customers said the food was cold. Warm dishes were sent out in ten minutes from the kitchen. At the end of the evening, Lucy breathed a sigh of relief. There were no great catastrophes and everyone was happy, including the mayor's two children who wanted larger burgers and a double portion of fries.

The next morning, Lucy's restaurant got a glowing review in the local newspaper from a food critic. The cherry on top of the cake was when, Lucy's Italian Restaurant was awarded five gold stars, by the Food and Restaurant Board in the city. Lucy was over the Moon, as that was something that meant a lot to her and to her parents, who had started the restaurant.

The Banquet that Never Ends

Just imagine if there was such a thing,
    A banquet with the most delicious dishes.
A table laid with the best food ever seen.
One that satisfies all your wishes.
There is a banquet that never ends.
It is not up there in the clouds,
It is not there up in the blue skies.
It is somewhere visible to human eyes.
Are you at this great feast?
It is a delight to all your senses,
It makes everything feel just fantastic,
It is not some complex magic trick.
In this banquet that never ends,
You find your family and your friends.
You find the best that life has to offer,
This life is your banquet that never ends.

The Global Banquet Project

Everyone open to thinking and behaving like a global citizen is welcome to take on this Global Banquet Project.

Let me first state that there are no strict rules as to who can and cannot take part in this project independently.

Here are the essential points to initiating the Global Banquet Project:

1. Choose members of your friends, family and colleagues who are like-minded individuals.
2. Select a date, time and venue.
3. Make a list of all the different dishes you are each willing and able to bring to the banquet.
4. Two, three or more people can come together to start their global banquet. Start as a small group and I am sure that the numbers will increase over time.
5. Prepare your food and bring it to the table to share.
6. Take the opportunity to share your cultural traditions, legends, folklore and everything you can bring to the table with your guests.
7. Create a global banquet community and share the knowledge with your circle, as newsletters, eBooks and presentations, for future generations to read and enjoy.
8. Find a purpose for your Global Banquet and make new goals for members of your Global Citizen community.
9. The Global Banquet can be held at any time, it is an

opportunity to come together to share stories and goodwill.
10. Build a collection of recipes for the food that was shared at the global banquet table. Share the Global Banquet experience using social media platforms, podcasts and videos.

Thank you for being an Ambassador of the Global Banquet Project and for sharing your experience as a global citizen.

Ideas for the Global Banquet Project

Create Themes around different Tables at different times of the Year

1. The New Year Global Banquet Table
2. The Christmas Global Banquet Table
3. The (Name of Country) Global Banquet Table
4. The (Name of Movie) Global Banquet Table
5. The (Name of a Music Group) Global Banquet Table
6. The (Name of an Actor) Global Banquet Table.
7. The (Name of a Season) Global Banquet Table.
8. The (Colour) Global Banquet Table
9. The Folklore Global Banquet Table.
10. The Myths & Legends Global Banquet Table.
11. The Wonders of the World Global Banquet Table.
12. The Guinness Book of World Records Global Banquet Table.
13. The Ripley's Believe It or Not Global Banquet Table.
14. The Twilight Zone Global Banquet Table.
15. The Global Comedians Global Banquet Table.
16. The World Leaders Global Banquet Table.
17. Save the Planet Global Banquet Table.
18. World Peace Global Banquet Table.
19. Nature, Flora & Fauna Global Banquet Table.
20. World Literature Global Banquet Table
21. World History Global Banquet Table.

THE GLOBAL BANQUET

GLOBAL BANQUET INVITATION FROM WARREN BROWN

Dear Friend, Reader & Fellow Writer

YOU ARE INVITED TO ATTEND ANY ONE OF THE LONG BANQUET TABLES TONIGHT

EVERY DAY — EVERY MONTH

YOUR IMAGINATION IS YOUR ENTRY TICKET

Don't miss out!

Visit the website below and you can sign up to receive emails whenever Warren Brown publishes a new book. There's no charge and no obligation.

https://books2read.com/r/B-A-LFGF-SPXHF

BOOKS 2 READ

Connecting independent readers to independent writers.

Did you love *The Global Banquet*? Then you should read *The Global Citizen*[1] by Warren Brown!

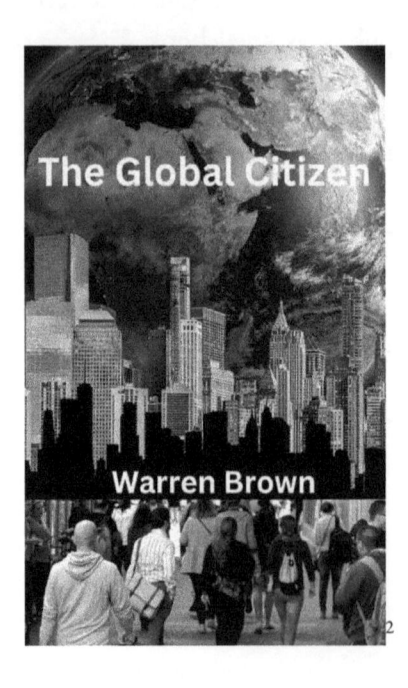

This is the age of the digital nomad. There are professionals travelling and working all around the globe, far away from their homes. These freelancers are comfortable in the countries that they visit. These entrepreneurs adapt to the land they live in as digital nomads. How are they able to live and work in an entirely new country?

Every country is so different and diverse from language, to food, customs, religion and social norms. After the pandemic life has changed for people and we are all learning to adapt to the new world of working. Will things go back to normal, or the familiar way that they were before the pandemic? I do not think so.

---

1. https://books2read.com/u/b5WOR7

2. https://books2read.com/u/b5WOR7

We live in a world that is more connected than ever before. The rise of technology and the ease of travel have made it possible for people to live, work, and thrive anywhere in the world. As a result, there has been a growing movement towards global citizenship - a lifestyle that prioritizes openness, diversity, and exploration. *There are so many videos on social media sites that inform and educate entrepreneurs to the fact that the age of "digital nomads" has arrived and it is here to stay.*

But what does it mean to be a global citizen, and how can you become one? In this book, I provide a step-by-step guide to help you live, work, and thrive anywhere in the world. I will cover everything from navigating legal requirements and finding housing to understanding local cultures and building community abroad.

Whether you are a young professional looking to build a career in a new country, a family looking to experience new cultures, or a retiree looking for adventure in your golden years, this book has something for you. I believe that anyone can become a global citizen, regardless of their background or experience. By following the steps in this guide, you can build a life that is truly global, filled with diverse experiences, new perspectives, and endless opportunities.

Read more at https://warren4.wixsite.com/warren.

Also by Warren Brown

Christmas Comics
The Father Christmas Factor
Christmas Legacies

Prolific Writing for Everyone
On Writing Magic
Universe of Creativity and Inspiration for Writers
Ocean of Ideas and Inspiration for Writers
Museum of Creativity and Inspiration for Writers
Doorways to Ideas and Inspiration for Writers
The Writer's Creativity Cave
The Writer's Oasis
Castle of Ideas and Inspiration for Writers
Chasm of Creativity and Inspiration For Writers
Island of Creativity and Inspiration for Writers

Standalone
Supernova: A Collection of Science Fiction Short Stories
Instant Poetry App
The Power of the Storyteller- A Collection of Short Stories

Vintage Tales: Eurasian Short Stories
Impostor Assassin
Camelot Crypto 1- Crypto Genesis
Camelot Crypto 2- Crypto Odyssey
Camelot Crypto 3- Crypto Symbiosis
Camelot Crypto: Three Short Crypto-currency Stories
Three Christmas Coins: A Poem
The Christmas Dimension
Happy New Year
Festive Delights
Coulrophobia: Empire of the Clown King
Creative Vibes
Rewrite Your Story To Become The Hero
Pandemic Blasters
New Year Odyssey
Pandemic Blasters Omnibus
Travel Man
Monkey in Mind
Masquerade
The Marauders and Mavericks
Mystic Inspiration Prompts for Writers
Cafe of Creativity and Inspiration For Writers
Quick Guide to Increasing Sales for Your Magnetic E-Book
The Global Citizen
The Mindset for Living in a World with Artificial Intelligence
Crowning of King Kang
Wild Ride
Storyteller's Toolbox
The Shangri-La Vacation
The Halloween Zombie Train
Humane Resources: A.I. Singularity
Civilization Rocks
New Year Magic

Bouquet for Earth
The Global Banquet

Watch for more at https://warren4.wixsite.com/warren.

About the Author

Warren Brown is an Author who has written in several genres from fiction to non-fiction. Warren is a certified Life Coach and Hypnotherapist. Warren completed his Advertising and Copywriting training through American Writers and Artists Inc. (AWAI). I have been an Indie publisher for over eleven years now. I have been writing and publishing on the web since 1993. Website:
    https://warren4.wixsite.com/warren
    Medium:
    https://warrenauthor.medium.com/
    Substack:
    https://warrenbrown.substack.com/
    Read more at https://warren4.wixsite.com/warren.

Milton Keynes UK
Ingram Content Group UK Ltd.
UKHW030950261124
451585UK00001B/84